CHILDREN'S
STORYTIME COLLECTION

The Sad Clown

AND OTHER STORIES

Contents

mustard

The Sad Clown

Bongo the clown had a bit of a problem. Clowns were supposed to be happy, funny, jolly people, but Bongo was a very sad clown. Nothing at all seemed to make him laugh.

Whenever the circus came to town people from all around flocked to the big top hoping for an exciting day out. They thrilled to the daring performance of the high-wire act, as the acrobats leaped from one swinging trapeze to the next. They enjoyed the jugglers, who tossed bright, sparkling balls into the air while standing on one leg. And the crowd delighted in seeing the beautiful white horses parading around the circus ring with the bareback riders balancing on their backs. When the seals came on, there was always a big cheer from the crowd, for everyone loved them and could watch their clever antics for hours.

But the biggest favourite of the crowd, especially with all the children, was the clown. Dressed in his big baggy trousers he would enter the circus ring with his funny walk. Everyone laughed to see him. They laughed even more when they saw his big floppy hat with the revolving flower on it. Even his painted clown face made them laugh.

But when his act started, the crowd thought they would burst with laughter. First of all his bicycle fell apart as he tried to ride around the ring. Then he fell out of his motor car when the seat tipped up. By the time he had accidentally poured cold water down his trousers and fallen into the custard-filled swimming pool, the crowd were almost crying with laughter.

But beneath all the makeup, Bongo the sad clown wasn't smiling at all. In fact, he saw nothing funny at all in bicycles that fell apart as you used them, or cars that tipped you out as you went along, or having cold water poured down your trousers, or even ending up face first in a swimming pool full of custard. He simply hadn't got a sense of humour.

All the other performers in the circus decided they would try and cheer the sad clown up.

"I know," said the high-wire trapeze acrobat, "let's paint an even funnier face on him. That'll make him laugh."

So that's what they did, but Bongo still didn't laugh and was still just as sad.

"Let us perform some of our tricks, just for him," said the seals.

So they sat on their stools and tossed their big coloured balls to each other, clapped their flippers together and made lots of honking sounds. But Bongo still didn't laugh. In fact, nothing that anyone tried made poor Bongo smile. He was still a very sad clown.

Then Percival the ring master spoke. "You know, I think I know what the problem is," he said. "There is nothing a clown likes better than playing tricks on other clowns. Perhaps if we had a second clown, that would cheer Bongo up."

So right away they hired another clown, called Piffle.

The circus arrived in the next town and soon it was time for Bongo and Piffle's act. Piffle started riding around on his bike while Bongo pretended to wash the car by throwing a bucket of water over it. Instead of the water landing on the car, of course, it went all over Piffle, who just happened to be cycling past at that moment. A little smile flickered across Bongo's face at the sight of the soaking wet Piffle.

Next, Bongo and Piffle pretended to be cooking, and Bongo tripped while carrying two huge custard pies. Both landed right in Piffle's face. Bongo let out a huge chuckle of laughter when he saw Piffle's custard-covered face.

At the end of their act, the clowns were pretending to be decorators, painting up a ladder. Of course, you've guessed it. The ladders fell down and all the pots of paint landed on the two clowns. Bongo looked across at Piffle, who had a big paint pot stuck on his head, with paint dripping down his body. Bongo threw back his head and roared with laughter. Piffle thought Bongo looked just as funny with paint all over his body, too. And as for the crowd – well, they thought two clowns were even funnier than one and they clapped and cheered and filled the big top with laughter. After that Bongo was never a sad clown again.

The Three Little Pigs

Once upon a time there were three little pigs who lived on a farm with their mother and father. They decided that, although they were just little pigs, they were quite grown up enough to make their way in the big wide world, so one day they set off together to make their fortunes.

After they had walked for quite some time, one of the little pigs started to feel rather tired. Just then, a farmer went by on his haycart.

"Hey, stop cart," the first little pig yelled. "You stronger brothers go on without me," he said. "This hay is light enough and soft enough for my house." And with that his brothers left the little pig with his pile of hay, and carried on their journey.

A little further down the road, the second little pig grew very tired. Just then, they passed by a forester cutting wood.

"Would you sell me some of your wood?" asked the second little pig. "This wood isn't too heavy and it isn't too rough for my house – it's just right." And with that the third little pig carried on his journey. Soon, even the third little pig grew very tired, and up ahead he spotted a builder making a wall out of stone.

"Aha," he thought, "that's exactly what I need to build my house, as it's strong and tough, just like me." And so he bought some stone and built himself a house.

That evening, just as the first little pig was settling comfortably in his bed of hay, he heard a rustling outside the house. He easily parted the hay with his hands to look outside, and gulped in fright when he saw the big bad wolf looking at him greedily.

"Little piggy, little piggy, will you let me in?"

"Not on the hairs of my chinny chin chin, I will not let you in," shuddered the first little pig.

"Then I'll huff, and I'll puff, and I'll blow your house down," said the big bad wolf.

And sure enough, he gave a little huff, and he gave a little puff, and with very little effort he blew the house down. Before the straw had settled to the ground, the little pig ran away as fast as his little legs would carry him to the home of his nearest brother.

The next evening, just as the two brothers were sitting down at their wooden table to eat their dinner, they heard scratching and sniffing outside the house. They peeked through the wooden window and gasped in alarm when they saw the big bad wolf staring at them hungrily. His stomach rumbled loudly.

"Little piggies, little piggies, will you let me in?"

"Not on the hairs of our chinny chin chins, we will not let you in," trembled the little pigs.

"Then I'll huff, and I'll puff, and I'll blow your house down," said the big bad wolf.

And sure enough, he huffed a bit, and he puffed a bit, and with a bit of effort he blew the house down. Before the planks of wood had crashed to the ground, the two pigs ran away as fast as their little legs would carry them to the home of their brother.

The next evening, just as the three brothers were making the fire to warm their toes, they heard crunching and crashing outside the house. The third little pig pulled a tiny stone out of the wall to make a peephole, and they all shrieked in terror when they saw the big bad wolf staring at them ravenously. His stomach grumbled even louder, and he was smacking his lips with glee at the feast waiting just a short breath away!

"Little piggies, little piggies, will you let me in?"

"Not on the hairs of our chinny chin chins, we will not let you in," quaked the three little pigs.

"Then I'll huff, and I'll puff, and I'll blow your house down," said the big bad wolf.

And sure enough, he took a big huff, and he took a big puff, and with a big effort he blew. But the house didn't blow down. So he took a bigger huff, and he took a bigger puff, and with the biggest of efforts he blew. But the house still didn't blow down. So he filled his lungs as full as he could and with a mighty effort he blew and blew and blew! And the house stayed up!

With that the big bad wolf started to climb up the stone wall to the chimney on the roof. The three little pigs looked around the stark stone room and then at each other in dismay – there was nowhere in here to hide, and nowhere left to run. They would have to stand and fight the big bad wolf!

Suddenly one of the little pigs had an idea, and whispered it into the ears of his brothers. They all ran over to the fireplace and hooked a huge pot of water over the roaring fire. They heard the wolf climb into the chimney. The water in the pot started to steam. They heard the wolf climbing down the chimney. The water started to bubble. They heard the wolf slide the rest of the way down the chimney and he landed splash in the middle of the pot of now boiling water. PLOP!

"AAARRRRI II II II II I!" screamed the big bad wolf, leaping immediately out of the boiling pot. The three little pigs ran around the room trying to get away from the wolf, as the big bad wolf ran around the room trying to cool down, until eventually he ran straight through the stone wall, leaving a huge big bad wolf shaped hole, and carried on running and screaming and shouting all the way through the woods. That was the last they ever saw of the big bad wolf.

The three little pigs knew they had beaten the wolf, and he would never trouble them again, so they decided to build a brand new, comfortable house to live in. They built the walls of tough, strong stone. They made tables of smooth, warm wood, and they gathered lots of sweet-smelling, soft fresh hay to make comfortable beds. It was the best house in the world, and they all lived in it happily ever after.

Granny Casts a Spell

Susie was very fond of her Granny. Each day, when Susie got home from school, Granny was always there sitting by the fire knitting. Granny knitted so fast that sometimes it seemed as though the knitting needles sparked in the firelight.

"Do you know," Granny would say, "that I'm really a witch?" Susie always laughed when Granny said that because she didn't look at all like a witch. She had a smiling face and kind eyes and she never wore black. Not ever. When Granny wasn't looking, Susie would take a peek inside her wardrobe just in case she might find a broomstick or a witch's hat. But she never found so much as a book of spells.

"I don't believe you're a witch," said Susie.

"I am," replied Granny, "and I'll cast a spell one day. You'll know when that day comes, for my needles will start to knit by themselves." After that, Susie kept a careful watch over Granny's needles, but they always lay quite still in the basket of knitting.

One day, Susie was playing in her garden when she heard the
sound of weeping. The sound seemed to be coming from under
the old tree in the corner. She walked towards the tree and as
she did so the crying noise got louder, but she could not see
anyone there. Then she looked down at her feet and there –
sitting on a mossy stone – was a tiny little man. He was neatly
dressed in a yellow velvet waistcoat and knickerbockers. On his
feet were beautiful, shiny, buckled shoes, and a three-cornered
hat with a wren's feather in it trembled on his shaking head.
When the little man saw Susie, he stopped crying and started to
dab his eyes with a fine lace handkerchief.

"Whatever can the matter be?" asked Susie, crouching down.

"Oh dear, oh dear!" sobbed the little man, "I am the fairy
princess's tailor and she has asked me to make her a lovely gown
to wear to the May Ball tonight, but a wicked elf has played a

trick on me and turned all my fine gossamer fabric into bats' wings. Now I shall never be able to make the princess's gown and she will be very angry with me." He started to cry again.

"Don't cry!" said Susie. "I'm sure I can help. My Granny's got a sewing basket full of odds and ends. I'll see if she's got anything nice for a party dress. I'm sure she won't mind sparing some – after all, you won't need much," she said. At that, the little man looked a bit more cheerful.

"Wait here," said Susie, "while I run indoors and see." She ran up the garden path and in through the back door.

"Granny, Granny!" she called. She ran into the sitting room expecting to find Granny knitting by the fire. But Granny had her eyes closed and she was whispering to herself. On her lap was her knitting – and the needles were moving all by themselves, so that the yarn danced up and down on the old lady's knees.

For a moment, Susie was too astounded to move. Then she thought, "I hope Granny's not casting a bad spell. I'd better make sure the little tailor is alright."

She ran back down the garden path and there under the tree sat the tailor, surrounded by a great pile of gorgeous gossamer, shining in the sunlight.

"I've never seen such fine material – ever!" he exclaimed. "But where did it come from? I just closed my eyes to dab them with my hanky and when I opened them again – there it was!"

"I don't know," said Susie, "but I think my Granny might have had something to do with it."

"Well, I'd never be able to thank her enough," said the tailor. "For now I shall be able to make the finest gown in the whole of fairyland. The princess will dance the night away in the prettiest dress there ever was." He paused and then went on, "I'm also indebted to you, for it was you who helped me in the first place. I would like it very much if you came to the May Ball, too."

"Why, thank you so much," Susie replied, "I should like that very much." She didn't want to hurt the tailor's feelings but she knew she couldn't go – she was far too big to go to a fairy ball!

"Well I must get on with the dress now," said the little man, reaching for a pair of fairy scissors. "See you tonight!" And with that he vanished.

Susie went indoors again. Granny was knitting by the fire as usual. Susie wondered if she had dreamed the whole thing. Everything seemed so normal. Really, how could she have imagined she'd seen a fairy tailor in the garden! And as for Granny casting a spell!

That night, Susie lay in bed and wondered if the fairies really were having a ball. How she longed to be there! Once she thought she heard a tapping at the window. Was that the fairy tailor she saw through the glass – or was she imagining it? In the middle of the night she awoke with a start. There was a click, clicking noise at the end of her bed.

"Granny is that you?" called Susie.

"Yes, dear," replied Granny. "I couldn't sleep, so I decided to do some knitting. All at once the needles started twitching, so I knew it was time to cast a spell. What is your wish, Susie?"

"I... I...," stammered Susie, "I want to go to the May Ball," she blurted.

"Then you shall, my dear," said Granny.

In an instant, Susie felt herself shrinking and when she looked down she saw she was wearing a beautiful gown and tiny satin slippers. Then she floated on gossamer wings out through the window and off to the Ball.

The next morning, Susie woke up in her bed. Had it all been a dream – the revelry, the fairy food, the frog band, the dance with the fairy prince? Then she saw something peeping out from under her pillow. And what do you think it was? It was a tiny, tiny shred of the finest gossamer fabric.

The Lost Lion

Once there was a lion cub called Lenny. He was a very tiny lion cub, but he was sure that he was the bravest lion in all of Africa. When his mother taught her cubs how to stalk prey, Lenny would stalk his own mother and pounce on her. When she showed them how to wash themselves, Lenny licked his sister's face instead so that she growled at him. When the mother lioness led her cubs down to the watering hole to drink, he jumped into the water and created a huge splash that soaked everyone.

The other lionesses were not amused. "You'd better watch that son of yours," they said to Lenny's mother, "or he'll get into really big trouble."

One day the mother lioness led her
cubs on their first big hunt. "Stay close to me,"
she said, "or you could get hurt."
She crawled off through the undergrowth with
her cubs following on behind, one after the other. Lenny was at
the back. The grass tickled his tummy and he wanted to laugh,
but he was trying hard to be obedient. So he crawled along,
making sure he kept the bobbing tail of the cub in front in sight.
On and on they crawled until Lenny was beginning to feel quite
weary.

"But a brave lion cub doesn't give up," he thought to himself.
And on he plodded.

At last the grass gave way to a clearing. Lenny looked up, and to
his dismay he saw that the tail he had been following was attached,
not to one of his brothers or sisters, but to a baby elephant!

Somewhere along the trail he had started following the wrong tail and now he was hopelessly lost. He wanted to cry out for his mother but then he remembered that he was the bravest lion in all of Africa. So what do you think he did? He went straight up to the mother elephant and growled his fiercest growl at her. "That'll frighten her!" thought Lenny. "She won't dare growl back!" And, of course, she didn't growl back. Instead she lifted her trunk and trumpeted so loudly at Lenny that he was blown off his feet and through the air and landed against the hard trunk of a tree.

Lenny got up and found that his knees were knocking. "Oh my," he thought, "that elephant has a very loud growl. But I'm still definitely the bravest lion in all of Africa." He set off across the plain. It was getting hot in the midday sun and soon Lenny began to feel sleepy. "I think I'll just take a nap in that tree," he thought, and started climbing up into the branches.

To his surprise, he found that the tree was already occupied by a large leopard. "I'll show him who's boss," thought Lenny, baring his tiny claws. The leopard raised his head to look at Lenny, and then bared his own huge, razor-sharp claws. He took a swipe at Lenny with his paw. Without even touching Lenny, the wind from the leopard's great paw swept Lenny out of the tree and he landed with a bump on the ground.

Lenny got up and found that his legs were trembling. "Oh my," he thought, "that leopard had big claws. But I'm still definitely the bravest lion in Africa." He set off again across the plain. After a while he began to feel quite hungry. "I wonder what I can find to eat," he thought. Just then he saw a spotted shape lying low in the grass. "That looks like a tasty meal," thought Lenny as he pounced on the spotted shape.

 25

But the spotted shape was a cheetah! Quick as a flash, the cheetah sprang away and as he did so, his tail caught Lenny a blow that sent him spinning round and round in circles.

When Lenny stopped spinning, he got up and found that his whole body was shaking. "Oh my," he thought, "that cheetah is a fast runner." Then he added in rather a small voice, "But I'm still the bravest lion in Africa." He set off again across the plain. By now it was getting dark and Lenny was wishing he was at home with his mother and brothers and sisters. "I wonder if they've noticed I've gone," he thought sadly as a tear rolled down his furry cheek. He felt cold and tired and hungry as he crawled into the undergrowth to sleep.

Some time later Lenny was woken by a noise that was louder than anything he'd ever heard before – louder even than the elephant's trumpeting. It filled the night air and made the leaves on the trees shake. The noise was getting louder and louder and the animal that was making it was getting nearer and nearer. Lenny peeped out from his hiding place and saw a huge golden creature with big yellow eyes that shone in the dark like lamps. It had a great crown of shaggy golden fur all around its head and its red jaws were open wide revealing a set of very large white fangs. How it roared! Lenny was terrified and about to turn tail and run, when the animal stopped roaring and spoke to him. "Come here, Lenny," said the animal gently. "It's me, your father, and I'm going to take you home. Climb up on my back, little one."

So Lenny climbed up on his father's back and was carried all the way home. And when they got there his father told his mother and his brothers and sisters that Lenny had been a very brave lion after all.

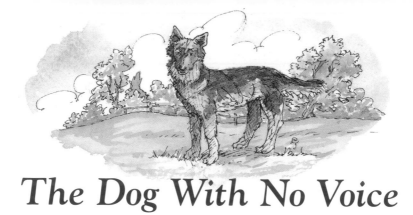

The Dog With No Voice

There once lived a prince whose words were pure poetry. He amused the court with his witty, rhyming verse, yet his kind and thoughtful words made him popular with all. It was said he could even charm the birds from the trees.

One day, he was walking in the forest when he came upon an old lady with a huge bundle on her back. "Let me help," said the prince. He took the load and walked along beside the woman. They chatted away and before long they had reached the old lady's door.

Now the old lady – who was really a witch – had been listening intently to the prince's words. "What a fine voice he has!" she thought to herself. "I would like my own son to speak like that. Then maybe he could find himself a wealthy wife and we'd be rich for ever more!"

"You must be thirsty," she said to the prince. "Let me give you
something to quench your thirst to repay you for your kindness."
The prince gratefully accepted, and was given a delicious drink
which he drained to the last drop. He was about to thank the
witch when he began to feel very peculiar. He found he was
getting smaller and smaller. He looked down at his feet and saw
two hairy paws. Then he turned round and saw to his horror that
he had grown a shaggy tail! He tried to shout at the witch but all
that came out of his mouth was a loud bark!

The witch hugged herself for joy. "My spell worked!" she
cackled. "Come here my son!" she called.

There appeared at the door a rough-looking young man.
"What's going on, my dearest mother?" he said in a voice that
sounded familiar to the prince. Then he looked down and
exclaimed, "Where did you find this poor little dog?"

Now the prince understood what had happened. "The old lady has turned me into a humble hound and given my voice to her son. Whatever am I to do?" he thought miserably. "I can't return to the palace. They'll never let a stray dog in." He turned with his tail between his legs and trotted off forlornly into the forest.

The witch and her son were delighted with his new voice. She made him scrub himself clean from top to toe and dressed him in the prince's clothes. "Now go," she said, "and don't return until you've found a rich girl to marry!"

The young man set off, eager to try out his new voice. Soon he was feeling very pleased with himself as he talked to passers-by. "What a very polite young man!" and "What a wonderful way with words," folk cried. "He could charm the birds out of the trees," other people said.

The witch's son travelled far and wide until at last he came to a castle where he spied a fair princess sitting on her balcony. He called to her and straight away she arose and looked down into the garden, enraptured by the sound of his beautiful voice. She was enchanted by his fine words and guessed they must belong to a prince. Soon the princess and the witch's son were chatting away merrily, and to his delight when he asked her to marry him she readily agreed. "For one with so beautiful a voice," she thought to herself, "must indeed be a fine young man."

Meanwhile, the poor dog-prince wandered in the forest, surviving as best he could by foraging for roots and fruits in the undergrowth. Feeling truly miserable, he stopped to drink from a stream. As he dipped his long dog's tongue in the cool water, he caught sight of someone sitting on a bridge. It was a pixie, fishing with a tiny net.

"Cheer up!" said the little fellow, "I saw everything that happened and I think I know how we can get your voice back. Follow me!" And with that he was off, dancing away through the forest with the dog-prince trotting along behind. They seemed to go on forever, and the dog-prince was feeling very hot, and the pads of his paws were quite sore, by the time they reached the castle. He could see the witch's son in the garden calling to the princess on the balcony. The dog-prince's eyes filled with tears, for she was quite the loveliest girl he had ever seen and he wished he could marry her himself.

"We will be married today," the witch's son was saying in the prince's voice, "I will await you by the church, my fairest one." Seizing his fishing net, the pixie leaped high in the air. As the words 'my fairest one' floated up to the balcony, he caught them in the net and gave them back to the dog-prince.

As soon as he had swallowed the words, the dog-prince could speak again. "Thank you, little pixie," he cried, "but what can I do? Now I am a dog with a prince's voice. The princess will never marry me."

"If you want to break the witch's spell, you must go to the church – fast!" said the pixie. And with those words he disappeared.

Straight away, the dog-prince ran to the church door. There was the princess looking most perplexed, for standing beside her was the witch's son – with not a word in his head. "I don't understand," she cried, "I thought I was to marry a silver–tongued young man, but now I find he is a dumb ragamuffin!"

"I can explain," exclaimed the dog-prince.

The princess spun around. "Who can explain?" she asked, for all she could see was a dog in front of her. "What a handsome dog!" she cried, bending down and kissing him on the nose. To her astonishment, the dog's hairy paws and shaggy tail immediately disappeared and there stood the prince. "But you're... but he..." she stammered looking from the prince to the witch's son.

Well, the prince explained everything that had happened, and after that he and the princess were married with great rejoicing. And as for the witch's son? He wasn't a bad young man, really, so the prince taught him to speak again – with a beautiful voice – and he married the princess's younger sister.

The Chocolate Soldier

In the window of Mrs Brown's sweet shop there stood a chocolate soldier. He had chocolate ears, chocolate eyebrows and a curly chocolate moustache of which he was particularly proud. But best of all he loved his shiny foil uniform with its braid on the shoulders and cuffs, and smart red stripes down each leg. All day long the chocolate soldier stood to attention on a shelf in the window, staring straight ahead out into the street. Standing next to him on the shelf were more chocolate soldiers, and beyond them he could see some sugar mice and a twist of liquorice bootlaces.

It was summer time and the sun shone through the window of the sweet shop. At first the chocolate soldier felt pleasantly warm; then he started to feel uncomfortably hot. Next he began to feel most peculiar indeed. His chocolate moustache was wilting and his arms were dripping. Soon he was completely melted and before he knew it, he had slipped out through a hole in his silver foil shoe and was pouring off the shelf and out into the street.

Down the street he poured.

"Stop! Help!" he shouted, but nobody heard his cries. Now he could hear the sound of gushing water and, to his horror, he could see he was heading for a stream at the bottom of the street.

"Help me! I can't swim! I'm going to drown!" the chocolate soldier cried as he plunged into the cold, running water. But now something very strange was happening. He found he could swim quite easily. He looked round and saw that he had a chocolate tail covered in scales. He looked down at his arms, but there was a pair of fins instead. The cold water had hardened him into the shape of a chocolate fish!

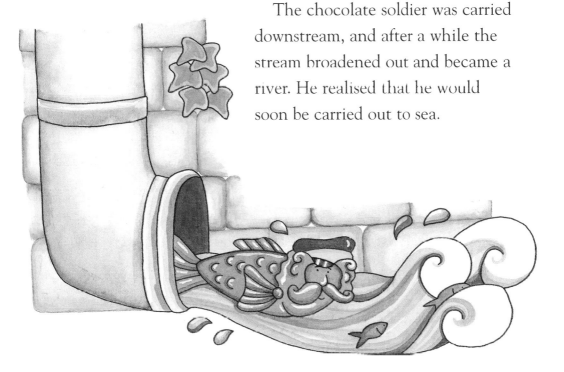

The chocolate soldier was carried downstream, and after a while the stream broadened out and became a river. He realised that he would soon be carried out to sea.

"Whatever shall I do?" wondered the chocolate soldier. "I'm sure to get eaten by a bigger fish or maybe even a shark!" He tried to turn around and swim against the river's flow but it was no good. The current swept him away down river again.

Soon he could see the waves on the shore. He smelt the sea air and tasted the salt in the water. Now he found himself bobbing up and down on the sea. He could see a boat not far away and then all of a sudden he felt a net closing around him. He struggled to get out, but the net only tightened and soon he felt himself being hauled out of the water and landed with a "thwack!" on the deck among a pile of fish. The smell was awful, and the chocolate soldier was quite relieved when he felt the boat being rowed towards the shore.

"I'll hop over the side as soon as we land and run away," he thought, quite forgetting that he had no legs but only a fish's tail.

But there was no chance of escape. As soon as the boat reached the shore, he and all the other fish were flung into buckets and lifted into a van. The van stopped outside a shop and a man carried the buckets inside, where it smelt of fried fish, chips and vinegar. The chocolate soldier found himself being lifted up with a lot of other fish in a huge metal basket. He looked down and saw a terrible sight below. They were heading for a vat of boiling oil! At that very moment he felt very peculiar once again. His scales melted, his tail drooped and he felt himself slide through the holes in the basket and into the pocket of a man's overalls.

The chocolate soldier lay in the corner of the pocket, while the man worked all day in the shop. Then the man headed for home, with the chocolate soldier bouncing up and down in the overall pocket as the man walked along. Soon they arrived at the man's house. He reached into his pocket.

"Look what I've found," he said to his small son. "A coin. Here, you can have it – but don't spend it all at once!" he said, chuckling to himself. The chocolate soldier felt himself being passed from one hand to another.

"So now I've hardened into the shape of a chocolate coin," he thought. "And I'm going to be eaten by the boy!" But to his surprise he found himself being slipped into the boy's pocket.

The chocolate soldier felt himself bouncing up and down in the child's pocket as he ran up the street and into a shop. The chocolate soldier peeped out and to his astonishment saw that he was back in Mrs Brown's sweet shop. Then he realised what was happening. The boy believed he was a real coin and was going to try and spend him! The boy stood in the queue at the counter.

The chocolate soldier called out to his soldier friends in the window, "Pssst! It's me! Help me get out of here!" One of the soldiers looked down, but all he could see was a chocolate coin sticking out of the boy's pocket. Then he recognised the voice.

"I'm a chocolate soldier like you, but I've been turned into a coin. Help!" cried the chocolate soldier.

"Leave it to me," replied the soldier on the shelf. "Don't worry, we'll have you out of there in a jiffy!"

The word was passed along and, quick as a flash, one of the sugar mice chewed off a length of liquorice bootlace. Then the soldier lowered the lace into the boy's pocket, where it stuck to the chocolate coin. Carefully the soldiers hauled the coin up on to the shelf. The chocolate soldier was delighted to find his foil uniform was still there on the shelf, just where it had been before. All the effort of getting on to the shelf had made him quite warm, and he found he could slip quite easily back through the hole in the shoe and into his uniform again.

"I'd like a chocolate soldier," said the boy to Mrs Brown. But when he reached in his pocket the coin had gone.

"Never mind," said kind Mrs Brown, "I'll let you have one anyway." She reached into the window and took down a soldier from the end of the row and gave it to the boy. And as for our chocolate soldier? In the cool of the night he turned back into a smart-looking soldier again.

The Wolf and the Seven Goats

There was once an old mother goat who had seven little goats. They all lived in a tiny house on the edge of a big, dark forest. One day, the mother goat had to go into the forest to collect food. Before she left, she called her seven little goats to her and said, "Now, children, promise me that while I am away you will lock the door and be on your guard against the wicked wolf. If you see him, don't let him in, because he would certainly eat you all up. You can recognize him by his gruff voice and his big black paws."

"Yes, mother," the little goats replied, "we promise to be very careful."

So the mother goat trotted cheerfully away into the forest, and the little goats locked the door. Some time later, there was a knock at the door, and the little goats heard a voice calling, "Open the door, children, it is your mother. I have brought back a present for each of you."

But the little goats heard that the voice was gruff, and not the gentle voice of their mother, and so they called, "No, we will not let you in! You do not have a soft voice like our mother's, you have a gruff voice. You are the wolf!"

So the cunning wolf went to a shop and stole a jar of syrup and swallowed it to make his voice soft. Then back he went to the little house by the forest. "Open the door, children," he called in his new, soft voice. "It is your mother. I have brought back a present for each of you."

Now the little goats heard the soft voice, but in his eagerness to get into the house the wolf had put his big black paws on to the window ledge, and so the little goats cried out, "No, we will not let you in! Our mother has beautiful white feet, but you have black feet. You are the wolf!"

So the wolf ran back into the village and went to the baker's shop, where he stole some flour and covered his paws in it. The wolf ran back to the little house by the forest. "Children, children, open the door!" he called again. "It is your mother. I have brought back a present for each of you."

The little goats heard the soft voice but they could not see any paws, and they called out, "Let us see your paws so that we know you really are our mother." So the wolf lifted up his paws, which of course were all white from the flour plastered on them. The little goats thought that this time it really was their mother, and they unlocked the door.

The wolf rushed in. The little goats screamed and tried to hide. One jumped into a drawer; the second squeezed under the bed; the third buried itself in the bedclothes; the fourth leaped into a cupboard; the fifth went into the oven; the sixth hid under a basin; and the littlest one slipped inside the grandfather clock. But the wolf found them and gobbled them up – all except the youngest one hiding in the grandfather clock. When the wolf had finished his meal, he felt very full and very sleepy. He wandered out of the house into a nearby meadow, lay down on some dry leaves, and promptly fell asleep.

When the mother goat came home from the forest, imagine
her horror as she saw the door open, the furniture strewn around
the house and the little goats all gone. She started calling them
by name, but nobody answered until she called out the name of
the youngest little goat, who was still hiding in the grandfather
clock. She quickly pulled him out, and then he told her what
had happened to all his brothers and sisters.

She ran out of the house with the little goat trotting beside
her and soon found the wolf sleeping in the meadow. She looked
carefully at him and saw that there were six lumps in his fat
stomach, and that they seemed to be moving. "My little goats
are still alive," she exclaimed with joy.

Quickly she sent the youngest goat back to her house for scissors, needle and thread. Then, while the wolf was still sleeping, she carefully cut a hole in the wolf's stomach. Soon a little goat popped out and then another and another, until all six were free and jumping for joy. They had not come to any harm, for in his greed the wolf had swallowed them all whole.

"Quick," cried the mother goat, "fetch me some rocks from the river so that I can fill up this wicked wolf's stomach." So the little goats each fetched a rock and the mother goat sewed them up inside the wolf's stomach.

When the wolf awoke, he was very thirsty. "What is the matter with me?" he thought. "I shouldn't have eaten all those goats at once. Now I've got indigestion." He set out to drink from the river. But his stomach was so heavy he could hardly walk and he staggered to the water's edge. As he bent over to drink, the weight of the stones pulled the wolf into the water, where he sank straight to the bottom and drowned. Then the mother goat and all her little goats – who had been watching – danced for joy. For never again would they be afraid of the wicked wolf!

This is a Mustard Book
Mustard is an imprint of Parragon

Parragon
Queen Street House
4 Queen Street
Bath BA1 1HE

Written by Derek Hall, Alison Morris and
Louisa Somerville
Illustrated by Anna Cattermole, Paula Martyr,
Julia Oliver, Martijn Orme, Charlie Anne Turner
and Kerry Vaughan

Printed and bound in Spain
ISBN 1-84164-022-0